"I love the way Greg and Mai told the story. This book is fun and fantastic. It will surely teach children to handle the 'stress and storm' of childhood with courage and confidence."

Umaporn Trangkasombat, M.D.
Professor of Child and Adolescent Psychiatry,
Faculty of Medicine, Chulalongkorn University

"Hilarious and heartwarming, it takes the reader on an exciting adventure ... It addresses some difficult subjects for kids -- bullying, exclusion, mockery. This book is collaboration between a Dad and his daughter, Mai, which transforms the family's worries about Mai's journey during her first year in a new school into fantasy adventure of quirky characters, sappy rhymes and clever raps. All this mirthful packaging makes it easy for kids to swallow, but no less meaningful."

David Doran, Founding Father, WeLearn.org

"You'd be surprised who needs help. Everyone needs help from time to time because everyone struggles."

Given the universal imperative above highlighted in Chapter 2, the authors have created a meaningful story that offers a lesson and words of wisdom for children and adults alike. A blend of whimsical storytelling merged with a fresh writing style will endear readers to the characters, while advancing the plot of an underdog neutralizing a bully and winning his friendship.

Chris Parker, Ed.M., Harvard

Snow Flake and the Big Race

Gregory Field Beatty
and
Natchariya "Mai"

Illustrations By: Colin Cotterill

Diary Illustrations By: Natchariya "Mai"

First printing, 2018

ISBN 978-616-478-382-9

www.snowflakeandthebigrace.com

Mai dedicates this book to her teachers at
The American School of Bangkok.

Be yourself, because the people who mind don't matter
and the people who matter don't mind.

—Dr. Seuss

CONTENTS

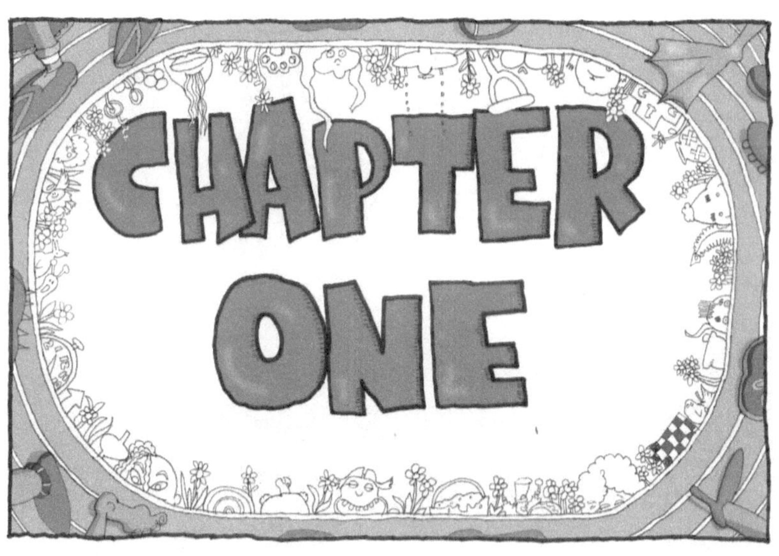

CHAPTER
ONE

A new school. A new beginning.

CHAPTER 1

A NEW SCHOOL YEAR BEGINS

THE BRASS BELL rang out from the top of the school like a cheering chime across the sky to welcome the students. The first day of the school year had begun.

Snow Flake wanted to look smart. She wore her favorite pale-blue pants, a spring green shirt, polka-dot socks, and ankle-high periwinkle sneakers.

Snow Flake entered her classroom. The desks were in three rows, with six desks in each row. She counted seventeen people—nine boys, eight girls. There was one empty desk waiting for her.

"Come in and sit down," said Mrs. Elms, the home-room teacher.

Snow Flake was careful not to rush to her desk. If she walked too fast, everyone would hear her slapping footsteps go, FLIP, FLAP, FLIP, FLAP. She walked slowly,

Snow Flake hopes that nobody notices her large shoes.

swaying left and right, lifting each foot as if she were wearing knee-high rain boots.

Mrs. Elms introduced the students to Snow Flake one by one. Last to be introduced was Cannon Ball. He was HUGE—the biggest boy Snow Flake had ever seen. It was as if a hippopotamus was sitting in her class.

"And this is Cannon Ball," said Mrs. Elms. "There is a rumor that last year Cannon Ball washed the windows of the school while he was in P.E. class. He wore an XL-size life jacket and did a belly flop into the pool. The splash went so high that it washed the windows all the way to the sixth floor of the school. The janitor was the only person happy about that."

Cannon Ball spoke up. "To add to the rumor, Mrs. Elms, my life jacket was not XL. It was XXL and it was three-proof."

"What do you mean by three-proof, Cannon Ball?"

"Waterproof, shark proof, and harpoon proof."

Mrs. Elms didn't know how to respond to that so she simply motioned Snow Flake to her seat.

Snow Flake sat in front of Mary Supial and one row over from Cannon Ball. Cannon Ball turned and stared at Snow Flake. She wondered if it was because of the way she walked slowly into the classroom. Of all the students, she did not want *this boy* to be the curious one.

Cannon Ball looked at her sneakers as he chewed his pencil. He bent down, and then he bent down further, so low that Snow Flake thought he might be trying to smell her sneakers. His nostrils flared with a sniff. He jerked his head back toward the front of the class as if he smelled something sour. Snow Flake took a deep breath and sighed.

Mary Supial leaned forward. She whispered, "Don't stare back at Cannon Ball. He is rude, crude, and full of bad attitude. He writes nasty hip-hop poems. Everyone is afraid of him, even the Grade 8 students. He gets the smarter students to do his homework for him and if they don't he threatens to punch them. And if he finds out your smart, he'll copy your answers during tests. He's a cheater. Be warned."

Mary observes the activities of all the students, good and bad, and writes them in her diary every day. She quietly passed her diary to Snow Flake showing her latest diary entry.

"Thanks for the advice, Mary," Snow Flake whispered as she passed the diary back.

Mary's diary entry #1.

Snow Flake thought that this might be the start of a friendship.

Snow Flake was worried about Cannon Ball, but her biggest worry was the swimming pool. The school had a sports stadium and an Olympic-sized indoor swimming pool with a high diving board. Swimming in *that pool* meant that all the other kids would see her feet. She wondered, *How can I swim in that pool and keep my oddball feet a secret?*

CHAPTER
TWO

CHAPTER 2

THERE IS NO CURE

SITTING IN DR. Fluffaluffer's office, the doctor told her, "There's no cure. No medicine. No magic potion. Not even a genie in a bottle could grant a wish for what you need."

Snow Flake had been teased by other kids all of her life. Being different was not fun. On many nights, she buried her face into her pillow and cried herself to sleep.

Her unusual name, Snow Flake, was no trouble at all. It was her feet. Worse than a scar, her feet were bizarre. She had rubbery webbed feet. The skin between her toes stretched from toe tip to toe tip. She was born with duck feet.

When she walked, her shoes slapped the ground: FLIP... FLAP... FLIP... FLAP. When she ran, she sounded like a car with a flat tire: flut, flut, flut, flut, flut, flut, flut.

"I haven't seen you for a while, so what's the reason for your visit this time?" asked Dr. Fluffaluffer.

"I'm having nightmares, terrible nightmares, and I'm grinding my teeth at night."

"What do you think is the reason for that?"

"I know exactly. During the summer we moved to a new neighborhood and I'm going to a new school. I'm worried that everyone will laugh at my feet and I'm afraid it's going to be worse than ever - the jokes, the name-calling, the talking behind my back."

Snow Flake caught her breath and started again. "The school has a huge pool, and when we have swimming lessons for P.E. everyone will see my feet. I can't wear my shoes in the pool so there's no hiding my feet. And there's a big kid who sits next to me and his name is Cannon Ball. I have to say, Doctor, and sorry that I'm not being polite, but he looks as destructive as his name. He sniffed at my shoes on the first day. One of the students told me he is an awful menace."

"Teasing is not new to you, Snow Flake. Kids can be cruel, you already know that."

Snow Flake slumped, and she looked exhausted. "Words may not break my bones, but they can sure break my heart."

"Well, we can't control how others treat you. But you do have one advantage. You've been struggling against this ridicule from a very young age."

"Huh?" Snow Flake shrugged her shoulders. "How is that an advantage?"

"You have an opportunity to overcome difficulties. You'll continue to learn ways to adapt. Everyone faces difficulties and difficulties get bigger as you get older. Struggling at a young age will make you stronger over time to face difficulties of all kind."

"But struggling gives me nightmares, not strength. That's why I'm here to see you today, Dr. Fluffaluffer. I feel so alone."

"That's another advantage you have, Snow Flake. Having nightmares tells me you have a strong imagination. That's a good thing. You'll be creative in your solutions."

"I'm not worried about being stronger or being creative. I'm worried about not being normal. All people want to do is point at me and talk about my weird feet."

"Well, you can't change your feet, you know that. The first step is to accept who you are and enjoy everything that is unique about you. You need to accept who you are before others accept you."

"The first step, Doctor Fluffaluffer, if you don't mind me saying, is to stop my nightmares. Do you have anything for that?"

"All you need is a double dose of Vitamin C."

"You mean drink two glasses of OJ in the morning?"

**Dr. Flufaluffer has no medicine to give Snow Flake.
Only encouraging words.**

"Not quite. Vitamin C…I mean courage and confidence…a double dose, Vitamin Courage and Vitamin Confidence… that's how you get better. That's how you stop the nightmares. It's all up to you."

"And just how do I become courageous and confident?"

"Helping others is a good way. A willingness to help others demonstrates a positive attitude, and it shows people you are a person of action. People notice helpers."

"Doctor Fluffaluffer, if you don't mind again, I'm the one who needs help. I'm the one here in your office."

"You'd be surprised who needs help. Everyone needs help from time to time because everyone struggles. Most people don't have the opportunity to practice overcoming difficulties like you. By overcoming obstacles, you gain strength. And people like success stories. Create your story, Snow Flake.

"Okay, Snow Flake, I think we're done now. To be crystal clear, the Vitamin C I'm talking about is not something you buy in the store. You find it within yourself, and if you find it, spread it around."

Snow Flake thanked Doctor Fluffaluffer on the way out. *Spread it around,* she said to herself over and over, thinking, *Spread it around, like its peanut butter...like I'm supposed to give Cannon Ball a peanut butter sandwich or something?*

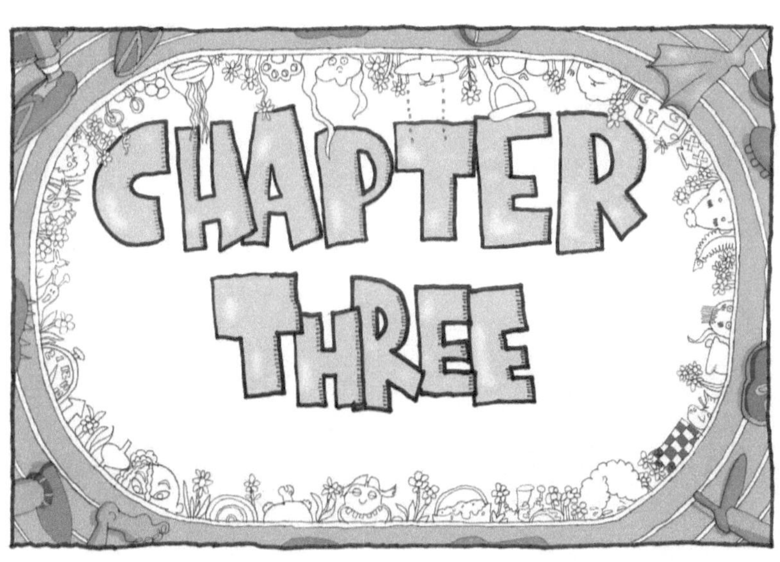
CHAPTER THREE

CHAPTER 3

SCIENCE CLASS

MRS. ELMS, THE home room teacher, taught science. She had the face of a kind grandmother. She was the oldest teacher at the school. Her hair was gray and woolly, as if a small poodle had been plopped upon her head.

"Science is our first class of the day," Mrs. Elms announced.

Snow Flake was thrilled. Art and P.E. were the favorite classes for ninety-nine percent of students, but Snow Flake was a one-percenter. She loved all things about science, especially chemistry.

While she was good at swimming, her passion was chemistry. She set up a chemistry lab in the basement of her new house.

Snow Flake got her first chemistry set on her eighth birthday, four years ago. She quickly became skilled with flasks, funnels, pipets, pinch clamps, ring clamps, goggles, toggles, droppers, beakers, bulbs and burets.

She made strange concoctions and healing powders. She called them *home remedies*. She believed her home remedies had cured her parents of stuffy snouts, burping bouts, and trouser shouts (it's a polite term for farts).

So far, no home remedy had cured her rubbery feet.

Mrs. Elms continued. "Today, we're going to learn about aerodynamics. Aerodynamics makes things go faster. Planes, trains and automobiles are designed to be aerodynamic."

This science class was not about chemistry. It was about shapes and designs. *There is nothing easy about aerodynamics*, Snow Flake thought. She had not even heard of this word before. It took her three times to spell it correctly in her workbook.

Mrs. Elms explained, "Aerodynamics examines the way air moves around things. By designing things aerodynamically, things go faster."

"Like what?" asked Mary.

Mrs. Elms responded, "High speed trains. Sports cars. Rockets. Even athletes, like swimmers and runners."

Snow Flake's eyebrows shifted upwards like two caterpillars sniffing the air. *Could aerodynamics help me run faster?* she wondered.

While Snow Flake daydreamed about aerodynamics, Cannon Ball focused on Snow Flake. It didn't take Cannon Ball long to make a hip-hop poem about Snow Flake. He

Aerodynamics makes things go faster.

bent toward her so only she could hear him. In deep, heavy breaths, he whispered a short, but forceful, threat.

> Your sneakers smell very strange
>
> I got a whiff at close range
>
> You hiding a secret from me?
>
> If I find out later, this I guarantee:
>
> The school bell will chime
>
> With a Cannon Ball rhyme
>
> Ding A Ling, Ring A Ding, Bong!
>
> Take a bath, face my wrath, Gone!
>
> Tell me now, life can be easy
>
> Tell me not, life shall be queasy
>
> For you!

As Cannon Ball turned away, he warned, "You're as sorry as your secret."

Tiny Dribbles noticed that Snow Flake's lip began to quiver.

"Hi, Snow Flake. Please allow me to introduce myself. I'm the smallest girl in the class, but you must know that already. Are you okay?"

"Hi, Tiny. Thanks for coming over. Mary warned me about Cannon Ball."

"The good thing about being small is that Cannon Ball never notices me and I get to eat all of my lunch. My house is next to his and he still doesn't notice me."

"What'd you say about your lunch?"

"I get to eat all of it. Cannon Ball never bothers me. For the other kids, he snoops around the cafeteria and looks to see who brought a tasty lunch. Then he just takes their lunch and tells them that if they complain to any teacher, he will give them a black eye."

"But he'll get kicked out of school if he hurts anyone, won't he?"

"He hasn't actually hit anyone yet; he only makes threats so far. But people know what he is capable of. I've seen him take the wings off of flies and feed the flies to his tarantula."

"What? He has a tarantula?"

"I've seen it. He brings it out in his back yard. It's hairy - there's even hair all over its legs. When Cannon Ball holds it in his hand, you can't see his hand. The spider is that big! He feeds it pond frogs and baby sparrows too."

"What? Baby birds? That's cruel."

"That's nothing compared to what he must do with stray cats."

"He kills them?"

"I haven't seen him do that, but I see all cats are frightened of him. They arch their back and go into hiding when Cannon Ball is around. That tells me he does something bad to them."

Snow Flake had now been warned twice. Once by Mary Supial, now Tiny Dribbles.

CHAPTER
FOUR

CHAPTER 4

ART CLASS

MRS. VAN LOBE taught art. She had an eye for beauty but was hard of hearing due to an unfortunate accident at a petting zoo.

The zoo had a goat with a long beard and two curly horns. Mrs. Van Lobe tugged at the goat's beard, thinking it would bring her good luck. However, her tug tickled the young goat, causing it to leap up with all four hoofs going sideways in the air. One hoof went, THUD, straight into Mrs. Van Lobe's left ear. She could no longer hear out of her ear, but the goat was fine.

The good news was that her loss of hearing had improved her other senses, especially her eyesight. She could see the potential of her students and she encouraged them to do their best. Her favorite phrase was, "Try, try, try your best, you'll be better than those who rest." The students loved her encouragement.

Mrs. Van Lobe gave the students feathered quills. "We're going to paint with these. These quills are special. They are not quills from ordinary birds. These quills have been plucked from black-bellied whistling ducks."

Junior artists at work. Creativity can be messy.

Snow Flake's face turned so white that her pupils appeared foggy gray. She was trying to keep her duck feet a secret. Now, in the first week of school, she and her classmates were using duck quills for painting! *Facts are crazier than fiction,* she thought.

Mary noticed Snow Flake's look of surprise.

"What's the matter, Snow Flake?" Mary whispered.

"I'll tell you after class, Mary. I trust you."

Cannon Ball saw the two girls chatting. "What's wrong, girls? You never saw a duck quill before? I've got lots of duck quills at home. And my dad has trophies from his duck hunting trips. My dad says the only good duck is a dead duck on a dinner plate."

"Our conversation is none of your business, Cannon Ball," Mary growled back.

Mrs. Van Lobe instructed the class. "We'll paint with watercolors and practice our brushstrokes. We're going to experiment and learn new ways to be creative. Being creative is the greatest way to feel alive."

The students dipped their quills in pots of paint and painted tops of pots and put spots on tops, greens with gray and gray with blues for different hues of blue.

Mrs. Van Lobe said, "Tickle the canvas with your feathery brush. Quills for thrills. Try new things. Surprise yourself."

Snow Flake put her blank canvas on the floor. She tossed colors on the canvas wherever her feather would fly. She whirled and hurled her feathery friend with a frenzy.

She tickled, tweaked, and twitched her body, spilling a rainbow of colors onto the canvas. For brush strokes, she tried thick ones, long ones, strong ones, short ones, splash ones, dot ones, fat ones, fine ones, quick ones, long-dash ones, and needle-thin ones.

She named her painting Feathered Friend by Snow Flake.

Cannon Ball stared at Snow Flake as if he had never seen such a creative style, probably amazed at the way she handled the duck quill so naturally. But he was not going to say anything nice.

Mary was right. Cannon Ball makes creepy poems.

Cannon Ball pointed at Snow Flake's painting. "Look, everyone," he shouted. "IT LOOKS LIKE SHE PUKED INSTEAD OF PAINTED!"

Snow Flake's face reddened, and she felt her cheeks warming. She tucked her chin into her shirt collar. She wished she could shrink to be as small as Tiny Dribbles.

Normally, a teacher would send a student to the principal's office for making a rude comment. But Cannon Ball always took advantage of Mrs. Van Lobe's hearing disability, and as a result, she did not hear Cannon Ball.

So, nothing happened, except Mary wrote it all down in her diary.

Mary's diary entry #2.

"Don't worry Snow Flake, I think your painting is cool," said Tiny Dribbles, putting her hand on Snow Flake's shoulder. Snow Flake lifted her head, smiled, and said, "Thanks, Tiny. You've got a big heart."

Cannon Ball used dark colors for his painting: black, charcoal grey, and brown. He had painted a housefly holding its head with his hands. He called it *Fly Scream*. On the back of his painting, he wrote a strange poem. The poem sounded like it came from *Jack and the Beanstalk*, except it was about how to eat a fly.

Mrs. Van Lobe said, "Lovely work, everyone. Take your paintings home. Put them on the kitchen fridge. Let your family enjoy your work!"

Snow Flake and Mary walked out of the class together.

"Snow Flake, I noticed you spilled paint on your shoes and I see your shoes are large. Does that have anything to do with what you want to tell me?"

"Can you keep a secret?" Snow Flake asked.

"Cross my heart."

"Mary …" Snow Flake paused. "I'm going to tell you something. Only you. You can't tell anyone. I really want to fit into this school and be treated normally. I want to be like everyone else."

"You can trust me."

"If anyone discovers what I am going to tell you, everyone will only see me as different…as weird."

"I can keep a secret. My diary has all my personal thoughts and I've never shown it to anyone, except you."

"Mary, I was born with duck feet."

"What do you mean?"

Snow Flake pulled Mary into an empty classroom. No one

could see them. Snow Flake quickly took off one shoe and sock.

"Holy crappers, Snow Flake!"

"Yup. My doctor said there is nothing I can do to change my feet. He said, 'Maybe you will find them useful someday.'"

"What are you going to do when we have swimming class in the pool for P.E.?"

"I don't know."

"Maybe I can help you. I don't know how, but I will keep this a secret."

Only time would tell if Mary could keep a secret.

CHAPTER
FIVE

MATH CLASS

MR. CALCULUS CLAY taught math. Mr. Clay's favorite phrase was, "Math is fun. It's not tons of fun, it's just sum fun." Heidi Harhar chuckled every time he said it.

Mr. Clay started every class by allowing Joe King to tell a math joke. Today, Joe asked the class, "Why is six afraid of seven?"

The class waited for the answer.

"Because seven ate nine." This joke was not one of Joe's best, and no one laughed except Heidi Harhar.

Cannon Ball stood up from his desk. "My favorite number is A-T-E." He spelled out the letters and rubbed his belly.

Mr. Clay said, "Cannon Ball, since you like food so much, let me quiz you with a math problem about food. If your right hand held twelve blueberry pies and your left hand held twelve raspberry swirls, and you balanced twelve pepperoni pizzas on the top of your head, what would you have?"

Mr. Calculus Clay makes math fun.

Everyone expected Cannon Ball to say thirty-six. But Cannon Ball said, "I would have breakfast, lunch, and dinner." Heidi laughed again. Even Mr. Clay chuckled. Then he started the multiplication lesson.

Mr. Clay wrote a math quiz on the board, but rather than write the quiz into her notes, Mary scribbled something in her diary about Cannon Ball's appetite.

Mr. Clay turned to the class. "Listen up. Today, I am going to teach you some math magic."

The class perked up, everyone at the same time.

Mary's diary entry #3.

"Pick any number. Keep it a secret. Don't tell me the number. You will put that number through my magic formula and I will guess your final answer. We're going to multiply, add, divide, and subtract."

"I'm tired already," said Cy Clops. His eyes were spinning. "I'm not good at math."

"No worries," assured Mr. Clay. "This magic math formula is easy."

"Mr. Clay, I like small numbers," said Tiny Dribbles. "Can I start with a number less than ten?"

"Sure," said Mr. Clay. "You can start with any number, small or large. Of course, the larger the number the harder it is to do the math, but the formula works with any number."

"Let's start," said the Katz twins together at the same time.

"Okay," said Mr. Clay. "Think of a number. Write it into your notebook. Don't show anyone."

Everyone wrote a number into their notebook.

"Now, double that number."

Everyone doubled the number in their notebook.

"Now, add six to that number."

Everyone added six to the number in their notebook.

"Now, divide the number by half."

Everyone divided the number by half in their notebook.

"Now, subtract the number you started with."

Everyone subtracted the number they started with.

"Your answer is THREE," exclaimed Mr. Clay.

Everyone gasped. No matter what number everyone started with, everyone had the same answer: THREE.

Cannon Ball said, "That is truly a magic formula, Mr. Clay, but I wouldn't want to do that with hamburgers. I started out with 15 and after putting it through your formula, I'm down to three."

Mr. Clay chuckled again, then wrote some harder math equations on the board. "I can assure you that if you learn all the math I teach, it will be just as dazzling as my magic math formula."

Mary whispered to Snow Flake. "Speaking of dazzling, wait until you meet our P.E. teacher, Coach Beefcake. He has the strangest beard."

CHAPTER
SIX

CHAPTER 6

P.E. CLASS

COACH BEEFCAKE TAUGHT P.E. He had bulging muscles and a long bushy beard. His beard hung from his chin like an upside-down bird's nest.

Mary rarely put funny stuff in her diary, but when she sketched Coach Beefcake, she drew a bat in his beard.

"While the weather is warm, we'll go outside. We're going running," said the coach.

Cannon Ball raised his hand. "Coach Beefcake, I don't want to run. I want to do sumo wrestling."

Coach Beefcake said, "Cannon Ball, sumo wrestlers are proud athletes that carry on a Japanese tradition. They are not wild beasts." Then he announced, "No wrestling. We're running. At the end of this month, we will run in the *Big Race*. We need to train for that. The three fastest runners in every class will be awarded gold, silver, and bronze medals."

Snow Flake thought about winning a gold medal. Then she looked down at her feet and thought about the impossible odds of winning.

Mary's diary entry #4.

Snow Flake was not going to give up just because she had duck feet. She remembered Mrs. Van Lobe's advice too. "Try, try, try your best." This seemed like good advice for everything, including running.

Cannon Ball looked over at Snow Flake and once again whispered so only she could hear.

You walk as slow as an ox

Jellyfish in your socks?

Squid in your shoes?

Tell me the news

Why they're big as canoes

Or I have a hunch

I'll eat you for lunch.

Squish, squash

Just you watch

Squish squash

Snow Flake slosh!

Jaws jamming, teeth gnashing, lips curling - onto
my tongue

Snow Flake sushi! Down in one gulp. Yum! Yum! - into
my tum

No salt, no pepper required

A Snow Flake Delight, I desire

Licking my lips 'til the very last chew

Then I'll spit your bones out...

For a stray dog's stew.

Snow Flake swallowed hard, like a python eating a porcupine.

Mary noticed Snow Flake was upset about something. She rested her hand on Snow Flake's shoulder. "Don't worry, Snow Flake, us girls will stick together."

Snow Flake may be slow, but she can beat that turtle.

"I was thinking the same thing during Mrs. Elm's science class. I wondered if my slowness was not just because of my duck feet but because of my heavy shoes too."

"Well, you can't just wonder, Snow Flake. You need to take action. You need to try on a pair."

"Where will I find aerodynamic shoes?"

"*Foot Candies.* I don't know if they'll have aerodynamic designs, but that shoe store always has the latest and greatest shoes."

"It's worth a try. I will talk to my parents about it tonight."

When the girls arrived at Snow Flake's house, Snow Flake invited Mary in to see her chemistry set.

Snow Flake took Mary down to the basement of the house. They passed through a door that had a sign.

CAUTION:

CHEMISTRY LAB

ENTER AT YOUR OWN RISK

"Wow, it's big. This is not an ordinary chemistry set. It's like a laboratory," said Mary. She studied the way the tubes twisted and coiled and then she looked across the room at a collection of colored jars. "What are those?"

The girls walked over to the jars.

"Those are the home remedies I've been working on." Snow Flake held each bottle up, one by one. "This is *Powdered Lizard Gizzards* for gout, this one is *Rattlesnake Shake* for shivers or shingles, this one is *Elephant Earwax Skin Cream* for sunburns and boils, and this one is *Gogol Mogul* with egg yolk for Yukon Yellow Fever."

Over several hours, Snow Flake showed Mary all thirty remedies that she was working on. She explained the ingredients of each one and the chemistry involved in the brewing process.

The two girls discussed home remedies to turn Cannon Ball into a kinder person, but they decided if he was going to change for the better, change would have to come from within himself. Snow Flake told Mary about Dr. Fluffaluffer's Vitamin C advice.

Mary suggested, "We need to do something different. We need to distract Cannon Ball during the *Big Race* so that he loses his concentration and finishes last."

"But how?" asked Snow Flake.

"We need to distract him with his favorite topic: FOOD."

Mary thought of a plan that seemed so simple, yet so genius. Snow Flake would have to be in the right place at the right time to make it work.

CHAPTER
SEVEN

CHAPTER 7

FOOT CANDIES

SITTING AROUND THE dinner table at home, Snow Flake said to her parents, "Mom, Dad, I need new shoes. Light ones. Shoes with an aerodynamic design. Shoes that wrap tightly around my feet."

Her parents stared back at her. They sat quietly, except for the munching sound from chewing their salad. *I'm getting the silent treatment again*, Snow Flake thought. This happened every time her parents thought her ideas were a waste of money or when they simply didn't understand. In this case, she thought they didn't know the importance of aerodynamics.

"Your shoes seem perfectly fine to me," her father said, breaking the silence.

"But, Dad, mine aren't aerodynamic."

"Mom. Dad. I need new shoes. Aerodynamic ones."

"I don't see the need to buy another pair of shoes. The ones you have are perfect. And they still fit."

"But they aren't perfect. They're too heavy." She sat up and raised one leg, putting her foot on top of the table. "You can see now. They're heavy."

"Hmmm," her father said, scratching the top of his head. "We can go to the store on the weekend. We'll have a look. But I'm not promising anything."

Snow Flake knew that "Hmmm" was her parent's code word for "No", but there was still one more opportunity to convince her parents. She would have to make sure they actually got to the store. And, hopefully, the store would have a pair of aerodynamic shoes in her size.

During dinner each night that week, Snow Flake reminded her parents of their promise.

"You know it's important for me to have good shoes, right? People only see me for my feet."

"Wait 'til they see how well you can swim. You'll be on the swim team for sure. Maybe captain of the team," said her father.

"Swim team?" Snow Flake huffed. "Dad, they'll laugh me right out of the pool. They'll ask me to be the team mascot, not the captain."

"Your over-sized shoes can hide reality only so long. You need to accept who you are and feel comfortable in your own skin," said her father.

Snow Flake knew better than to get in an argument with her father, especially when she needed him to pay for a new pair of shoes. *I just want the pain to go away and be normal*, she thought.

When Saturday arrived, she woke up early. She cleaned her bedroom and helped with household chores. She even cooked scrambled eggs for her parents. All this effort was to ensure her parents were in a good mood.

After breakfast, they drove to *Foot Candies*, the local shoe store. At the store, her father spotted a bin of shoes piled high as a mountain. A large sign above the bin read:

Clearance Sale

Last Year's Design

70% Discount

Must Sell

Snow Flake's father sorted through the bin with great energy, picking up several pairs. He held up one pair with a smile. "If we have to buy another pair of shoes, let's get these ones. These ones have strong support around the ankles."

Snow Flake's jaw dropped. "Dad, those are winter hiking boots."

"They're perfect," he said.

Her father could not have picked a worse pair. Snow Flake had to find a proper pair, and fast. She saw a shelf with a sign that said the following:

Just Arrived

All New Designs

She picked a pair that was bright yellow, with a black **V** logo. "Dad, this pair looks full of aerodynamics," she said.

Her father walked over and picked them up. He held them in his hands. "There's no doubt about it, these are light," he said.

Snow Flake let out a sigh of relief. It seemed like her father finally understood the importance of aerodynamics.

Snow Flake's father went on. "They may look cool, and maybe you can run fast in them, but they don't have any support around the ankle. The other shoes I picked out are better."

New shoes to help Snow Flake run faster.

The salesman, who had overheard their conversation, walked over to Snow Flake. He explained the benefits of the new design. He spoke loudly to make sure Snow Flake's father heard every word.

"Great choice," the salesman said to Snow Flake. "These are the fastest pair of shoes we have in the store. The only way to make you run faster would be to put scorpions in them."

"Do you have a pair in my size, without scorpions?" Snow Flake asked.

"We sure do," the salesman said with a wide grin.

Snow Flake was still not sure if her father understood the importance of aerodynamics but he finally agreed to buy the pair she wanted. Snow Flake walked out with a new pair of bright yellow running shoes with a black **V** logo.

She would soon find out if they would make a difference.

CHAPTER
EIGHT

CHAPTER 8

THE ACCIDENT

SNOW FLAKE AND the other students continued to train after school. They ran on the school track, practicing short, medium, and long distances. Her new shoes felt light, but at the end of each lap she still finished last. Her new shoes didn't make her run faster.

Worst of all, the bright yellow color attracted more attention from Cannon Ball. He laughed at the sight of her bright yellow shoes.

"I knew there was something strange about your feet," Cannon Ball puffed. "I looked at them on the first day when you tiptoed into class. The way you walked was strange. Now I know. Your feet are way too big for your body. They look even bigger in yellow sneakers. They look like yellow submarines."

He rapped a short ditty.

Grippery, slippery, slock

Yellow sub 'round her socks

Navy of one

Soon to be drowned

Slow fishy! Snow fishy! Shock!

Snow Flake wondered if she should cancel her plan to distract Cannon Ball during the *Big Race*. Maybe it was too crazy to work. *And if it does work, he's going to be super angry*, she thought.

Another week passed.

Coach Beefcake announced that the class would have a practice race. The students were excited. It was a chance to see how everyone would perform in a competition. Snow Flake wondered how she could compete without running like, well, a duck.

The girls lined up at the starting line. All nine of them bent down, their upper bodies leaning forward in the ready position.

"We'll go one time around. One lap." Coach Beefcake raised his arm high in the air. "ON YOUR MARK, GET SET, **GO!**"

On the first corner, Snow Flake was even slower than the short-legged Tiny Dribbles. Her heart pounded hard like a hammer. Her new shoes pounded on the track, flut, flut, flut, flut, flut, flut.

At the second corner, she moved up one spot, passing Tiny Dribbles. Snow Flake was in eighth place. She thought that maybe the shoes were helping her to run faster. *These shoes are built for racing*, she thought.

Something terrible happened on the third corner.

Tiny Dribbles was catching up to Snow Flake. Snow Flake turned her head to see Dribbles. Snow Flake lost her balance, her right ankle twisted, she tumbled, and she landed hard on the track.

This is not a good day. Everyone knows Snow Flake's secret now.

She looked down at her right ankle. It was swelling up like a balloon. Her eyes squeezed in pain. Coach Beefcake and Cannon Ball ran over to Snow Flake. Tiny Dribbles was in tears, crying harder than the injured Snow Flake.

Coach Beefcake bent down to take off her shoe and sock.

Cannon Ball's eyes nearly popped out. Snow Flake's foot, with no shoe and no sock, had him in shock.

Cannon Ball turned to the classmates and exclaimed, "SHE'S GOT DUCK FEET. I KNEW SHE WAS HIDING SOME-THING." Everyone ran over to look.

Coach Beefcake must have been surprised about Snow Feet's duck feet too. His eyes opened wide as he held his hand around the swelling ankle.

Cannon Ball said, "I overheard Snow Flake talk about her crazy chemistry experiments. She must have swallowed one of her own freakish home brews." He started to laugh. The other kids started laughing too, except Mary and Tiny, who were worried for Snow Flake. Mary sketched something in her diary.

Coach Beefcake lifted Snow Flake into his arms. A loud **SNAP!** crackled from his chest.

Coach Beefcake scrunched his face. He bent down to let Snow Flake slide out of his grip. His right hand reached around to hold his side. He took a deep breath, bent down again, lifted Snow Flake up, and carried her to the nurse's office with determination.

As Coach Beefcake took Snow Flake away, Cannon Ball was still booming with laughter. He gathered the class-mates around and started to rap.

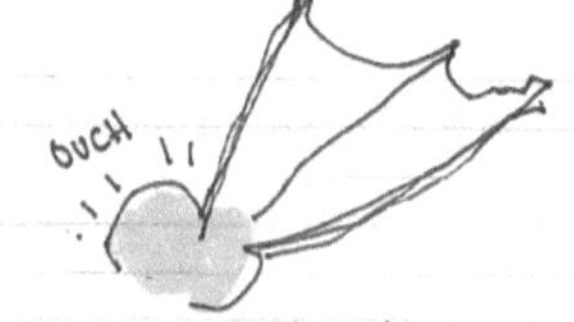

Accident !!

Snow Flake sprained
her ankle. She is in pain.
I think she cannot run in
the Big Race.
   I must be honest in
my diary.
      It's truly strange.

She has duck feet !!
Cannon Ball laughed and
made the other kids laugh.
He is a jerk again

Dreadful.

Mary's diary entry #5.

I've seen her without her shoe,

This girl belongs in a zoo,

She's not human! More like a bird!

Her three-toed feet are truly absurd.

She'll never win medals, not even bronze,

She'll have more luck catching fish in a pond.

She chanced not to tell me the news

This awful sight, inside of her shoes

Flip, flop, flap, last 'round the track

I could win in a potato sack

I could have SAVED HER from this shame

For this sad outcome, she is to blame.

While Cannon Ball created a comic calamity with the other students, Snow Flake and Coach Beefcake needed serious medical attention.

Nurse Betty, the school nurse, took a look at Snow Flake's foot. At first, Nurse Betty looked startled at the sight of Snow Flake's foot, but it didn't take her long to know what was wrong. "Sprained ankle," said Nurse Betty.

The nurse looked over at Coach Beefcake. He was bent over, gasping with short breaths.

"And what is your problem, Coach Beefcake? You're breathing in and out like a broken accordion," the nurse said to him.

"I think I broke a rib lifting Snow Flake. The same one I broke last year. It never healed properly."

Fixing ribs and ankles.
Just another day at the office for Nurse Betty.

"Oh dear. Another gym teacher who thinks he's Tarzan, tossing around students like they're chimpanzees. Let me have a look."

The nurse poked and probed his chest and stomach. Once again, it didn't take her long to know what was wrong. "Broken rib."

"How bad is it?" he asked.

"Don't lift anything heavy for a month. In fact, don't lift

anything at all, except for a knife and fork for your dinner. I'll wrap these bandages around your chest and you can be on your way."

The nurse wrapped his chest. Coach Beefcake nodded, agreeing to follow the nurse's instructions.

As he was leaving, Nurse Betty said it one more time. "Coach Beefcake, no lifting for one month. No exceptions."

Coach Beefcake bowed his head again. "Thanks, Nurse Betty."

The nurse returned her attention to Snow Flake. She wrapped Snow Flake's foot with bandages and gave her a pair of crutches. "You'll need these for ten days."

Snow Flake's heart sunk to the pit of her stomach. The *Big Race* was in seven days.

CHAPTER
NINE

CHAPTER 9

THE BIG RACE

THE FIRST PART of Snow Flake's plan was to get healthy. She went to visit Nurse Betty every day for therapy. Every night, she slept with bags of ice wrapped around her foot to make the swelling go down.

Seven days passed. The swelling was gone! Even though Nurse Betty had told Snow Flake to use the crutches for ten days, Snow Flake felt strong enough to run in the *Big Race*.

"I have never seen anyone make such a fast recovery. Seriously, it's a miracle," said Nurse Betty. Snow Flake just smiled and said, "Thanks for your help, Nurse Betty."

What Snow Flake didn't tell Nurse Betty was that she had been drinking one of her home remedies for the past seven days. This concoction was to make her healthy quickly and give her extra energy.

Mary was the only person she told. With Snow Flake's permission, Mary wrote the recipe in her diary. If it worked, they could brew it together and sell it. This was Part 1 of her plan. Part 2 was to happen during the *Big Race*.

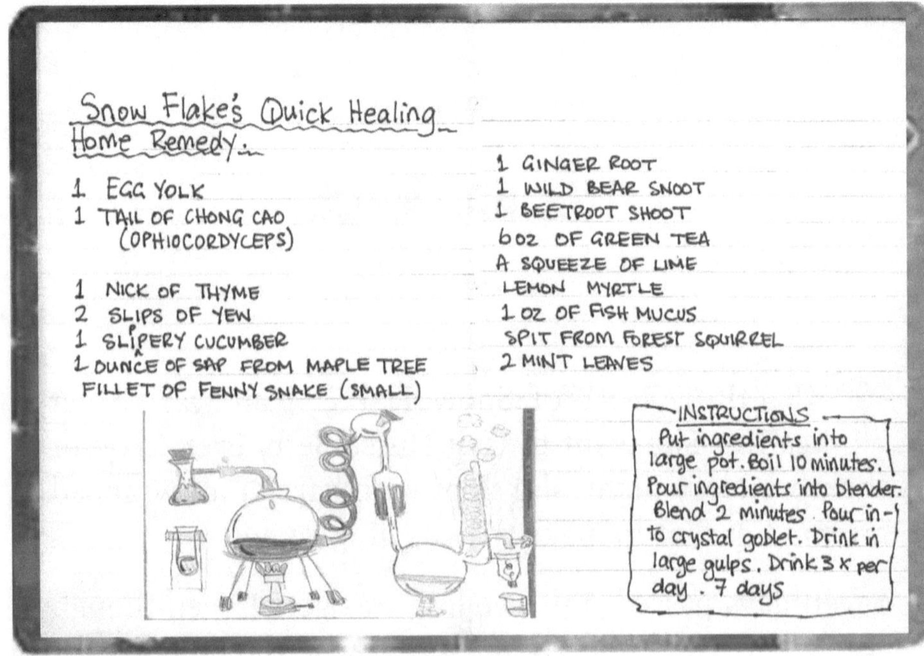

The big day arrived. Students, parents, relatives, friends, important people, and local celebrities all gathered in the stadium. The sun was shining. There was not one cloud in the sky but there were strong gusts of wind. Mrs. Elms' hair ruffled in the breeze, as if it were a beehive buzzing with honeybees.

There was a carnival-like atmosphere. People were buying hot dogs, cotton candy, and sugary drinks. People were waving hand-held flags. It was loud and noisy. Even Mrs. Van Lobe could hear the cheers from the crowd.

Students from kindergarten to Grade 8 were in their racing shorts and sports shirts, stretching with excitement. Tish Hughes had photos of her dog, Spot, who had recently died from swallowing a bucket of spot remover, printed all over her shirt to honor his memory.

Snow Flake wore a tight shirt, running shorts, and a baseball cap, worn backwards to hold her hair down. Nurse Betty wrapped her ankle for support and glued her toes together. Snow Flake felt aerodynamic from head to duck toe.

Over the loudspeaker system, the stadium announcer, Froster Hewitt, welcomed everyone to the *Big Race* and announced the rules for the day.

"Welcome to the *Big Race*. This is the day we've been waiting for all year. The students from each grade will race against their classmates, with boys and girls racing together. Grades 1-5 will run 100 meters. For Grades 6-8, each race will be two laps of 400 meters, for a total of 800 meters. Gold, silver, and bronze medals will be awarded for first, second, and third place.

"Races will start with the kindergarten students and we will work our way up to the Grade 8 students."

Snow Flake looked out at the oval track. She didn't expect a gold, silver, or bronze medal. But if she tried her best, and her homebrew worked, maybe she could finish in the middle.

Froster Hewitt announces the Big Race with a big voice.

Cannon Ball shouted over to her. "Hey, Snow Flake, how are your Franken-feet? Did they let the animals out of the zoo today?" Then he shouted another rap ditty.

Icky dicky duck, we need a garbage truck

Tricky dicky truck, to collect this ugly duck

Get in the truck, you three-toed duck

Our school will cheer, sneer, and smile

As you quack a mile to the city trash pile!

Snow Flake ignored him. She was only thinking about her plan.

It was time for the Grade 7 students to race. Snow Flake and her classmates lined up at the starting line. They looked nervous. Tiny Dribbles' knees rattled together. Cy Clops' eyeglasses steamed up. Roy Rash and Roy Wayne, both of whom collected wristwatches for a hobby, kept setting and resetting the stopwatch function on their Irish and Swiss wristwatches. Anna Conda looked tense too like she might cough out a rabble of butterflies.

Froster Hewitt looked down from his booth, ready to announce the runners and do the play-by-play.

Coach Beefcake stood at the starting line. He saw the runners were in place. He looked up at the announcer. Froster Hewitt signaled a *thumbs up*. Coach Beefcake raised his arm. "ON YOUR MARK, GET SET, GO!"

Froster Hewitt started to announce the race.

> "They're off. Astor Nott rockets to the front, creating space between him and Tish Hughes. Willie Catcher and Betty Wont are right behind. Will he catch her? I bet he won't. But no one knows; we're only at the start of a two-lap race.
>
> "I see three runners falling behind. Cannon Ball, Snow Flake, and Tiny Dribbles are in the final three spots. Cannon Ball is already breathing heavy. I hear a flut, flut, flut sound from Snow Flake's shoes.
>
> "As the runners move into the first turn, Roy Rash is catching up to the front four. He has come out of nowhere, as most rashes do. He's followed by another Roy, Wayne Roy. Roy Wayne and Roy Rash are neck and neck in fifth and sixth.

The weather is fine, but there's a tongue twister out there, with the two Roys running hip to hip.

"Closing in on the front six runners are the Katz twins, Bob and Kitty Katz. All the other runners—Cy Clops, Anna Conda, Dee Bends, Farley Fahast, Mary Supial, Joe King, and Heidi Harhar—are bunched up at the turn. This is a disappointing start for Farley Fahast, who's usually first and fairly fast, but Farley Fahast is not first, he's eighth.

"They're in the far straight away, still on the first lap. It's Astor Nott in the lead, but Roy Wayne and Roy Rash have moved into second and third.

"Challenging Tish Hughes for fourth are the Katz twins. With the dogs on Hughes' T-shirt, we've got Katz and dogs in the race today.

"Betty Wont has moved into eighth. Two-eyed Cy Clops is breaking away from the back of the pack. He's in ninth. But he'll have to keep an eye out for Anna Conda, who has also slithered her way out of the pack. She's in tenth. Cy Clops, who is keeping one eye on Anna Conda, is looking strong.

"In the back ten, it's Bends, Supial, King, Harhar, and still further back, it's Cannon Ball hopping along and Snow Flake flapping along. Tiny Dribbles is trailing at the end.

"Here we go into the second turn. The front

runners remain the same, but there is some movement in the back ten. Here comes Joe King. Behind King is Heidi Harhar. The two of them running together—Joe King and Heidi Harhar—is no laughing matter. King is in eleventh and Harhar is in twelfth.

Huffing and puffing all the way to the finish line.

"Cannon Ball is huffing and puffing. Snow Flake shows a determined look but she's still at the back, with no flurry, only flutter, as if her yellow shoes are greased with butter. Tiny Dribbles is trailing at the end.

"As they come into the first turn on lap two, the top six remain the same. In seventh, it's Willy Catcher, and Betty Wont is in eight. Here comes Anna Conda. She's weaving in and out of the other runners. Will she catch Willy Catcher? She does! She sneaks her way past Willy Catcher and Betty Wont, and now Anna Conda is a mere sneeze away from Tish Hughes. Conda passes through! Conda is now in fourth!

"More action in the middle of the pack. Coming out of the pouch is Mary Supial. She's challenging Dee Bends. Mary is coming on strong. Mary goes 'round Dee Bends. Mary Supial is in seventh. Fahast is still in eighth. Cannon Ball and Snow Flake are in the back. Tiny Dribbles is trailing at the end.

"Down the far straightaway. Heidi Harhar is turning it on. All joking aside, she's passing Joe King on the inside and she smiles at King on the way by. Cy Clops clips by Catcher and clops his way past Wont too. There's no question, Willy Catcher is falling further back. He's gassing out quickly. Cannon Ball too has his mouth wide open like he's trying to catch flies.

"They move out of the final turn. The final one hundred meters. The crowd is on their feet. Everyone is cheering. Here come the runners!

"At the finish line, it's Astor Nott for the gold, followed by Roy Wayne for the silver and Roy

Rash for the bronze. Several runners are bunched up in a pack as they cross the line—it's too close to call. There are still three more runners to cross.

"Five meters from the finish line, Snow Flake has a burst of energy. She's right beside Cannon Ball. She leans toward him."

**Snow Flake, Cannon Ball,
and Tiny Dribbles trailing at the end.**

Froster Hewitt put his mouth close to the microphone. "It looks like Snow Flake is shouting something at Cannon Ball."

"Look," Snow Flake said to Cannon Ball. "Look at the man selling hot dogs up in the stadium."

Cannon Ball spotted a man with a tray of hot dogs. Cannon Ball lost his concentration. His eyes were no longer fixed on the finish line but were pointing up to the stadium. He was now thinking about the wonderful taste of a dozen frankfurters, loaded with cheeses of cheddar, feta, and brie; a medley of mustards, whole grain, stone ground, and brown; sauces of chimichurri, piri piri, and chop suey soy; peppers pickled, chili, sweetened, and green; and honey, chutney, and dill.

Faster than the food fantasy passing through Cannon Ball's mind, Snow Flake passed Cannon Ball.

"It's Snow Flake finishing sixteenth, Cannon Ball seventeenth, and Tiny Dribbles trailing at the end."

The runners hovered around the finish line catching their breath. Nurse Betty walked over to inspect the runners to make sure they were okay.

Snow Flake raised her arms in victory.

Mary pulled out her diary which she wore on her kangaroo belt. This was the most important event of the year—history in the making. She wrote down everyone's name in the order they finished. Instead of interviewing the medal winners first, she ran over to Snow Flake for her first interview.

Snow Flake still had her arms raised in victory.

"Snow Flake, you finished sixteenth, but your plan worked. You distracted him. You beat Cannon Ball."

"Yeah, the second part of our plan worked. I beat the nastiest boy in the school! It's a personal victory."

Cannon Ball cranked his head toward Snow Flake. He clearly overheard her. "I can't believe you tricked me. I will seek revenge," he threatened. He rolled out another hip-hop tune.

> Revenge! Revenge! Is now my aim
>
> You put my reputation to shame
>
> Enough of your duck feet shenanigans
>
> I'll make sure you'll never run again

For the first time since her first day in class, Snow Flake was scared. Cannon Ball had a talent for hip hop, but his words were hurtful. *He's a destroyer, not a builder,* she thought.

CHAPTER
TEN

CANNON BALL GOES DEEP

SEVERAL WEEKS PASSED. The warm weather turned cooler and so did Cannon Ball's attitude. Every time Cannon Ball saw Snow Flake, he grunted like a bear.

After school one day, Cannon Ball and Joe King were walking home together. Cannon Ball turned to Joe. "Hey, Joe, I know you like jokes and pranks. Can you keep a secret?"

"I think so," said Joe. In fact, Joe was not good at keeping secrets. Everyone knew his password was P-A-S-S-W-O-R-D. But if there was ever a reason to keep a secret, it would be to not do anything to make Cannon Ball angry.

"Snow Flake tricked me during the *Big Race*. I'm gonna get revenge."

"Maybe I can help. I know some good duck jokes."

"Try one on me."

"Knock, knock."

"Who's there?"

"Robber."

"Robber who?"

"Robber duck. Hand over your valuables!"

"Revenge needs more than a bad duck joke, Joe. I am going to prank her. I'll borrow my father's duck whistle that he uses for his hunting trips. The next time we're swimming in the school pool, I'm going to invite every duck in the neighborhood. The pool will be full of ducks! Everyone will think the ducks came to play with Snow Flake."

"You should bring your giant water gun too," suggested Joe.

"Good idea. It's the size of a hunting rifle. Yup, I'll see how much that duck likes water. I'm gonna soak her good." A smile spread across Cannon Ball's face. "Joe, can you keep another secret?"

"Okay."

"I'm going to fill my gun with dirty, smelly, stinky, frowzy, putrid pond water."

"Yikes," said Joe, "sounds dirtier than my dirtiest jokes and smellier than my worst joke."

Cannon Ball's plan for revenge was timely. A few days after his talk with Joe King, the P.E. class moved indoors. Indoor P.E. classes meant it was time for swimming lessons.

The students stood around the pool in their swimsuits and towels waiting for Coach Beefcake.

Cannon Ball thought this was a perfect time to do his prank. He snuck over to his gym bag. He reached in, pulled out his father's duck whistle, a water gun, a large sheet of heavy paper, two strips of sticky tape, and a large red pen. He wrote **"QUACKERS"** on the paper in large red letters.

Cannon Ball plays his pranks.

As Cannon Ball walked back to the group, he blew his father's duck whistle.

Cannon Ball reached over to Snow Flake, slapped her back and said, "I love farm animals."

Before Snow Flake could see what was on her back, Coach Beefcake arrived. He sat down on a bench by the pool to begin his lesson on pool safety.

Luckily for Snow Flake, Mary and Tiny were standing beside her. They reached over together and pulled the sign off and tossed it to the ground. Coach Beefcake never saw the sign on Snow Flake's back.

Several ducks arrived as Coach Beefcake taught his lesson. He could not see the ducks since he was giving his lesson and facing the students, but he must have heard a few giggles, the loudest coming from Cannon Ball and Heidi Harhar.

Heidi Harhar's laughter had the high pitch of a hyena, which was a good thing because it scared the ducks and they flew away before the swimming started.

Cannon Ball's water gun was strapped behind his back, so Coach Beefcake did not see that either.

Coach Beefcake told the class to settle down. "Let's get into teams of two. Pair up. One boy, one girl."

Everyone stated pairing up, though each boy seemed to shy away from Snow Flake. Cannon Ball seemed more interested in his water gun than selecting a partner. He walked over to his towel to hide it before Coach Beefcake saw it. Cannon Ball and Joe King communicated to each other with a wink.

It appeared no girl wanted to be Cannon Ball's partner.

Coach Beefcake said, "Snow Flake, I bet you're a strong swimmer with your webbed feet. Can you please be Cannon Ball's partner?"

Snow Flake's heart pounded in her chest. She was the only person remaining without a partner. She had no choice but to accept Cannon Ball as her partner. Coach Beefcake did not know about Cannon Ball's nasty behavior and she was not about to explain it now in front of Cannon Ball.

The students started to get into the pool. Cannon Ball sat at the edge of the pool. He ignored Snow Flake. He looked at the water with a strange look on his face, like he had just seen a box of eels released into the pool. He slowly shuffled into the shallow section.

Snow Flake climbed up the ladder of the three-meter diving board.

Snow Flake walked out to the tip where it was most springy. She bent down to touch her hands to the diving board. She placed her fingers around the edge of the board and straightened her body into a handstand. Her body was motionless. Her hips, knees, and legs were in a perfect line. Her duck feet looked larger than ever, pointing up.

Everyone looked at her.

Nobody blinked.

They waited for her to dive.

Snow Flake pushed herself off, tucked into a summersault, and did a double twist on the way down. **"PERFECT ENTRY!"** Coach Beefcake shouted.

Everyone clapped as hard as they could—except for Cannon Ball. He continued to move slowly in the pool. This was his first time in the pool without his life jacket. He wasn't familiar with where the drop in the pool was where the shallow section became the deep end.

Perhaps it was gravity, perhaps it was because the bottom of the pool was slippery, but Cannon Ball suddenly slipped into the deep end. His feet scuffled for grip. The faster his feet scuffled, the faster he moved deeper into the water.

The waterline went from his waist, to his chest and then to his neck. His eyeballs circled wildly as if the imaginary eels had shot an electric current up his spine. **"COACH BEEFCAKE! I CAN'T SWIM!"**

It was the last thing he said before his head went under the water.

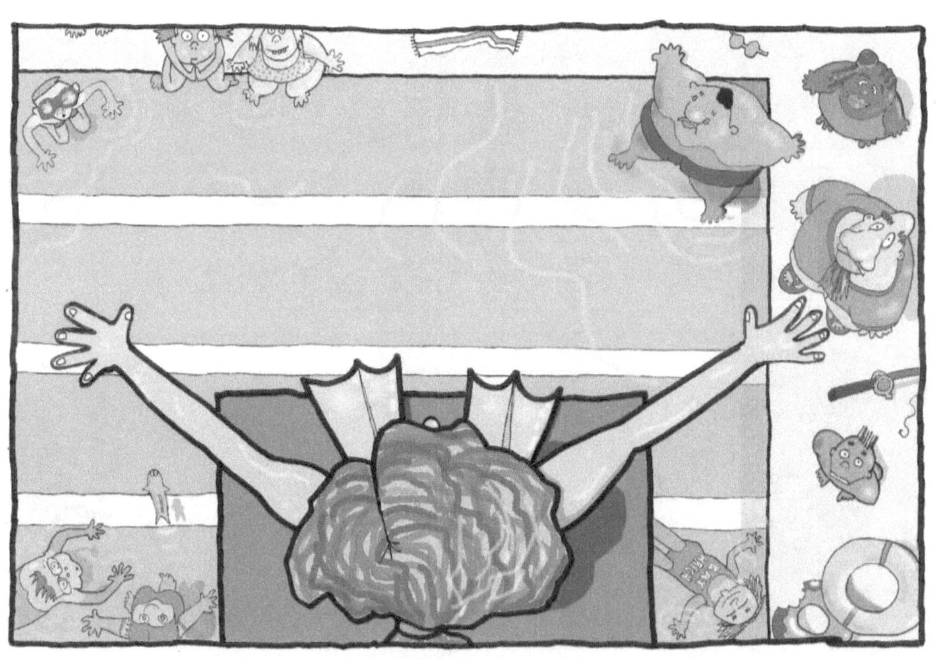

Snow Flake feeling confident and on top of the world.

"Excuse me while I show off a little bit."

CHAPTER
ELEVEN

CHAPTER 11

THE SEA LION

COACH BEEFCAKE TOOK off his shirt and raced toward the pool. He looked like a moving pile of boulders, except for the bandage wrapped around his chest.

"Coach Beefcake," Snow Flake shouted. "Nurse Betty's instructions! Remember? I was there. You agreed. You're still injured."

A worried look ran across Coach Beefcake face.

"You won't be strong enough to lift Cannon Ball out of the pool," Snow Flake said.

Coach Beefcake yelled to Mary, "Call the fire department. They have long rescue ladders."

"Let's drain the pool," one student suggested. Another student shouted for someone to bring a large fish net.

Anna Conda reached in with her long rope-like arms, but Cannon Ball was too heavy to lift.

Snow Flake said calmly, "Coach Beefcake, I think I can save him."

"How do you like my duck feet now, Cannon Ball?"

Coach Beefcake looked down at Snow Flake's feet. "Snow Flake, I knew you had special feet for a reason. I really hope you can swim like a duck. Please save him."

Snow Flake fanned her webbed toes, spreading them wide. She took a deep breath. Her chest expanded. She dove in and swam to the bottom of the pool. Her duck feet moved fast. All anyone could see was a streak of bubbles moving toward Cannon Ball. She reached out to put her arms around his legs. She lifted him. Her feet fluttered with torpedo speed like motorboat propellers. She carried him to the edge of the pool.

Coach Beefcake and all the boys grabbed Cannon Ball's arms and lifted him to the side of the pool. Their faces turned tomato red as they struggled to lift him. It took all the effort of the boys to lift Cannon Ball.

Cannon Ball lay flat on his back at the side of the pool, catching his breath.

Snow Flake climbed out.

The class roared. They cheered. They clapped. The class rushed over to Snow Flake and put their arms around her.

"Snow Flake, you are a HERO," Coach Beefcake shouted.

Snow Flake bowed her head. "No, sir, I am not a hero. I just used some good Vitamin C, courage and confidence. One of my new home brews. But this one is from the heart instead of my chemistry lab."

"Well, Snow Flake, I'm not sure what you mean by Vitamin C, but your natural ability saved Cannon Ball. If you weren't different, Cannon Ball would have drowned. You saved him. How good is that?"

Cannon Ball caught his breath. He got up and walked slowly toward Snow Flake like a wounded sea lion. "You saved my life, Snow Flake. Thanks. I'm sorry I called you many nasty names."

Snow Flake didn't say anything.

Cannon Ball tucked one hand behind his back and crossed

his fingers. He reached out with his other hand to rest it gently on Snow Flake's shoulder. Standing in front of her, he made up a short hip-hop ditty.

You saved me from drowning

I will stop my nasty clowning

Sorry I've been so rude

I want to be your dude

Your uniqueness

Is your sweetness

Snow Flake was pleased with Cannon Ball's kindness, but she wondered, *Can one act of kindness really mean a person can change for the better? Did this bully suddenly become like the Grinch whose heart grew three times the size on Christmas day? Should I accept his apology?*

Mary ran to get her diary to write down this moment. Her hand was shaking as she wrote the words. Mary made a double entry in her diary to capture this moment. She wasn't sure if Snow Flake should believe Cannon Ball.

HARD TO BELIEVE ..

(but I saw it with my own eyes and heard it with) my own ears. After Snow Flake saved Cannon Ball, he looked at her with puppy dog eyes. He made up a nice poem with rhymes. First time I heard him say something sweet. But somehow

I don't believe him. I think he crossed his fingers behind his back when he said it. Not sure. He may have just been scratching his butt.

Anyway, I need to warn Snow Flake.

Mary's diary entry #7.

Q. WILL CANNON CHANGE TO BECOME A BETTER PERSON?
- ☐ yes
- ☐ no hope. Always dreadful
- ☑ undecided.
- ☐ needs more time - maybe forever.

Mary's diary entry #8.

CHAPTER
TWELVE

FINAL WORDS

BEFORE THE CLASS was dismissed, Coach Beefcake spoke up. "Attention, everyone. I have something important to say."

The class gathered around Coach Beefcake, but not too close, in case things crawled out of his beard.

"Today, we saw how being different is a good thing. Snow Flake may never win a race, but *because of her feet*, she saved Cannon Ball. Our *differences* make us special."

Coach Beefcake stroked his beard as if searching for a good thought. "Think about how each of *you* can be different. Not just physically different, but different by doing new things that interest you. Be original. Don't only follow what your friends do. Be a leader."

Mary piped up. "Mrs. Van Lobe taught us that in art class. I wrote it in my diary." She flipped through her diary to the correct page and said, "Try new things and try, try, try your best, you'll be better than those who rest."

"Yes. And dare to be different," said Coach Beefcake.

Coach Beefcake paused for a moment. "Think about Mrs. Van Lobe. She can't hear too well, but she can see talent. Mrs. Elms has fuzzy hair, but her heart is clear and kind. Mr. Calculus Clay tells silly jokes, but he knows how to make math fun. And look at me. I've got the biggest muscles and bushiest beard in the school."

"I think I saw a squirrel in it the other day," said Joe King.

"I think I saw a bat in it. And it was hanging upside down. I sketched it in my diary," Mary said. The class laughed. Coach Beefcake laughed too.

"Coach Beefcake, can I say something?" Snowflake asked.

"Of course!"

"Coach Beefcake, your beard really quacks me up!"

The class roared with laughter. Heidi Harhar giggled and jiggled so hard she nearly fell backwards into the pool.

"I'm glad you like my beard, Snow Flake, and all the critters inside it," said Coach Beefcake. "We need to be able to laugh at our differences too."

Joe King stepped forward. "Hey, Coach, if you want a laugh, I've got a joke. Knock, knock."

"Who's there?"

"Walter."

"Walter who?"

"Walter Gun. CANNON BALL'S WALTER GUN." He pointed to Cannon Ball's towel. "Under that towel he's got a water gun. He planned to soak Snow Flake with his water gun filled with icky, dirty, smelly pond water."

"Hey, Joe. That was our secret. That was my plan *before* Snow Flake saved my life," pleaded Cannon Ball.

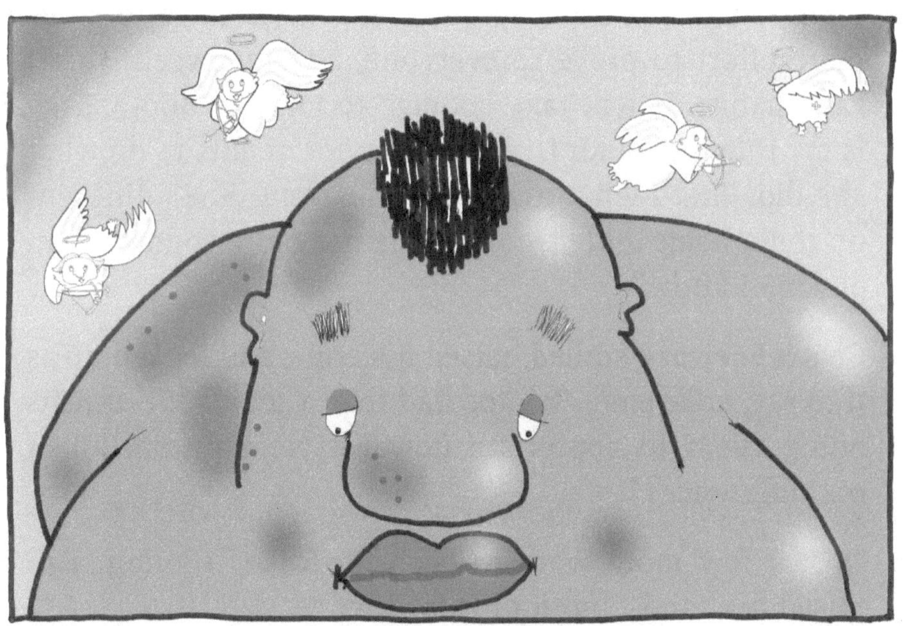

Cannon Ball eats humble pie.

"Oops," Joe said, realizing his blunder. "I just meant to tell a good joke."

"Well...I'm kind of glad you told that joke. Now I have a chance to explain in front of everyone the reason my plan for revenge has changed."

Cannon Ball started his announcement by looking into the eyes of each of his classmates, slowly turning his head to make eye contact with everyone. He clasped his hands in front of his body.

"I've been a bully. I've pestered Snow Flake since the first day she arrived. I've pestered a lot of other people too. When I think of how I've acted, I feel horrible."

Cannon Ball's bottom lip quivered. "I will have to show more effort to prove to everyone, and to myself, that I can change. It will take courage to change. Snow Flake is my role model for that. It took a lot of guts to do what she did. That's what makes her different. She's different on the outside *and the inside*. She has more courage than anyone I know."

Coach Beefcake smiled, raised his arms, and looked up as if to say, *halleluiah*. "It's too bad that it took a life-threatening event to appreciate how we benefit from all of our differences."

"Just a few more words, Coach Beefcake." Cannon Ball raised his hands, motioning for silence.

"I'm a big person on the outside. I can dominate with my size and strength. But dominating is not the same as leading."

Cannon Ball bowed his head further. "I'm small on the inside. I've never had to struggle, like Snow Flake. I've been a destroyer, a taker. I've never learned to be a builder, or a giver. That takes strength from the inside. I don't even know how to make friends. I really don't.

No one wanted to be my partner for swimming. My only true friend is my tarantula. But I'm going to try to be a builder."

Snow Flake moved a step closer to Cannon Ball. "The first step for you to show us how you're going to change is for you to learn to swim. I'll teach you if you teach me how to write a friendly hip hop poem. No mean ones."

Everyone cheered at the thought of Snow Flake and Cannon Ball helping each other with their talents. Coach Beefcake dismissed the class, and the girls lifted Snow Flake onto their shoulders and carried her to the girl's locker room.

On the way home, Snow Flake reflected on her time since arriving at her new school. She fit in faster than she thought was possible, and she was hopeful that Cannon Ball was going to become a better person, and a better swimmer. She thought, *This is better than winning a gold medal in the Big Race.* She could hardly wait to tell Dr. Fluffaluffer that Vitamin C was spreading around.

STUDENT PROFILES

Major Characters

Snow Flake

Snow Flake is a new student at the school. Her desire is to fit in by being normal. She loves science and has a passion for chemistry.

Cannon Ball

Cannon Ball is the class bully. He is a talented rapper too. Most of his rap ditties are mean. He is big which also makes kids scared of him.

Mary Supial

Mary Supial observes the activities of all the students, good and bad, and writes them in her diary every day. She carries it in a pouch on a belt made of kangaroo hide. She hops on breaking news. She pulls her diary and pen from her pouch faster than a gunslinger with itchy fingers.

ntermeDiate characters

Joe King

Joe King loves to tell jokes. He is the class clown, schoolyard fool, and jolly buffoon. His favorite jokes are *Knock, knock* jokes. Example: *Knock, knock. Who's there? Frank. Frank who? Frank you for laughing at my jokes.*

Heidi Harhar

Heidi Harhar brightens the class with her hardy laughs. She laughs loudest at Joe King's jokes, especially his *Knock, knock* jokes.

Tiny Dribbles

Tiny Dribbles is the smallest person in the class, as her name suggests. She also has the biggest heart, proving good things do come in small packages.

Minor characters

Dee Bends

Dee Bends is the strongest girl in the class. She can do the most push-ups, pull-ups, sit-ups, and hiccups of all the students.

Willy Catcher

Willy Catcher is a good baseball player. Coach Beefcake, the P.E. teacher, says Willy hits home runs every time and he catches everything that comes his way. This must be true because he catches colds easily too. He snorts and sniffles all year round.

Cyril Clops

Cyril Clops is Bob and Kitty Katz' cousin. His nickname is *Cy*, named after the one-eyed mythical creature. But Cy has two eyes, and wears thick glasses, giving him the appearance of four eyes.

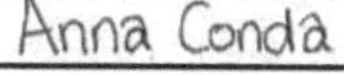

Anna Conda

Anna Conda likes to give smothering hugs. Her arms are long, like firehoses, and she squeezes tight!

Farley Fahast

Farley Fahast is fairly fast and likes to be first. He is first to arrive at school in the morning, he is first to finish his homework, and his birthday is January 1, the first day of the year.

Tish Hughes

Tish Hughes cries a lot. Most recently, it's because her dog *Spot* died. Strangely, he died by jumping into a bucket of spot remover. It was to be used to clean the carpets at the Hughes' home. The bucket was marked *Hazardous Liquid*, but Spot could not read.

Bob Katz

Kitty Katz

Kitty and Bob Katz are twins. They also have twin Siamese cats, named Herman and Sherman. Sometimes people call Herman "Sherman" and Sherman "Herman", but the two Katz and the two cats all know that Sherman is Sherman and Herman is Herman.

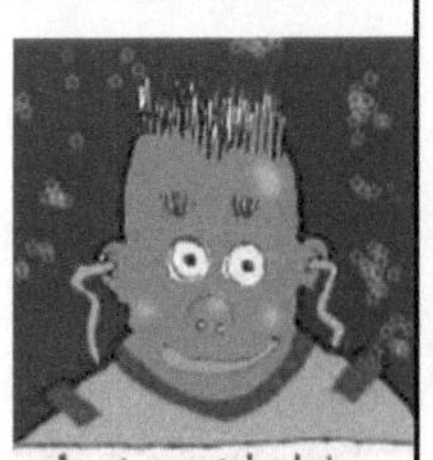

Astor Nott

Astor Nott wants to be an astronaut. He wants to be a sailor of the universe, walk on lunar landscapes, and meet Buzz Lightyear. He plans to travel to the sun and says he can do this without getting burned if he travels at night.

Roy Rash

Roy Wayne

There are two boys in the class named Roy: Roy Rash and Roy Wayne. They have an interesting hobby. They collect watches from around the world. Roy Rash has an Irish wristwatch and Roy Wayne has a Swiss wristwatch. That's not easy to say fast, but Farley Fahast says it fairly fast.

Betty Wont

Betty Wont is determined to do well in everything she does. She is always positive. One time a teacher showed her a glass half-filled with water. The teacher asked if the glass was half full or half empty. Betty said, "It doesn't matter because it's a beautiful glass."

ACKNOWLEDGEMENTS

Greg would like to thank:

This book started as a family exercise, a six-page story that I wrote for Mai. As I read it to her, she insisted on changing some events, certain words, and the ending. The story grew longer as we worked on it together. When we decided to turn the story into a book, I realized we needed help.

I am grateful to Colin Cotterill, illustrator extraordinaire, for assisting with more than the illustrations. When reading early versions, he insisted we expand several sections, now in the book, particularly the *Big Race* play-by play. As for the illustrations, he brought the characters to life. Colin visualized each character, without my assistance. The unsolicited humor that he snuck into the illustrations made Mai and I chuckle, too. I thank him for his initiative as much as his artistry.

I thank our eclectic team of reviewers, who ranged in age from seven to seventy-something. Courtney Broderick McCormick, Jim Sullivan, Pam Wilkie, Chris Parker, Ham

Brower, Eliora Olshansky (USA); J.D.M. Stewart, Carly Jeffs, the Werkman family: Darcy, Dominque and Braxton (Canada); Roger Sherlock (USA and Thailand); Akari Kishi (Japan); Daniel and Christian Zelealem (Ethiopia); Youssef and Ahmed Mansi (Egypt and Dubai); Sathya Chan (Cambodia and Myanmar); Alex Harrop (England and Thailand), the Bangkok Triplets of Trip, Trey and Troy Ruenprapan (Thailand); Alice Jin (China and Thailand); and Oliver Alexander (Australia). Their criticism and encouragement were equally stimulating.

Mai would like to thank:

This story took more than two years to complete. I would like to thank my dad for coming up with the original story, reading the many versions of it to me, and for agreeing to most of the changes I suggested - some of the characters and things that happen to them. I definitely did not want Snow Flake and Cannon Ball to be girlfriend and boyfriend at the end. He needs to take good care of cats too.

AUTHORS AND ILLUSTRATOR

Greg Beatty was born in Canada but is now a long-term resident of Thailand. He is an international business executive, with a Juris Doctorate from New England School of Law and a BA in Administrative Science from Colby College. This is his first book.

Natchariya "Mai" is in Grade 5 at the American School of Bangkok. This is her first book.

Colin Cotterill is a London-born teacher, crime writer and cartoonist. He lives in Thailand, where he writes the award-winning Dr. Siri mystery series and the Jimm Juree crime novels.

9 786164 783829